My
Great-Grandpa Joe

Marilyn Gelfand · *photographs by* Rosmarie Hausherr

Four Winds Press
Macmillan Publishing Company • New York
Collier Macmillan Publishers • London

Macmillan Publishing Company
866 Third Avenue, New York, NY 10022
Collier Macmillan Canada, Inc.
Printed in the United States of America

10 9 8 7 6 5 4 3 2 1

The text of this book is set in 14 pt. Palatino.
The illustrations are black-and-white photographs
reproduced in halftone.

Library of Congress Cataloging-in-Publication Data
Gelfand, Marilyn.
My great grandpa Joe.
Summary: Spending a memorable Sunday with her great
grandfather and her other grandparents, eight-year-old
Deborah realizes that with health, the elderly can lead
rich and varied lives.
[1. Grandparents—Fiction. 2. Old age—Fiction]
I. Hausherr, Rosmarie, ill. II. Title.
PZ7.G2784My 1986 [E] 86-2044
ISBN 0-02-736830-0

To my dear family and all those
who surround me with their love
—M.G.

*F*irst thing this morning, I remember something special. It's Sunday, and right after breakfast we are going to visit my great-grandpa Joe.

I love going to Pappa Joe's, but my brother, Kenny, would often rather stay at home with his games and his computer. Sometimes Mom lets him, but not today. At breakfast, Mom tells Kenny, "No excuses, because we're going to see great-grandma Sarah too."

Pappa Joe and Grandma Sarah have been married a long time, but now Pappa Joe lives in an apartment by himself and Grandma Sarah lives in a nursing home nearby. I can't remember her very well.

Suddenly, I don't feel very hungry.

"Don't worry," Mom tells me. "We'll only stay with Grandma Sarah a little while and then we'll come home for a big Sunday lunch with all your grandmas and grandpas."

It takes over an hour to drive to Pappa Joe's apartment building. Kenny and I run up the front steps and ring the bell.

Pappa Joe answers through the intercom and buzzes us in, and we all ride the elevator to the twenty-sixth floor. It's a long way up. Pappa Joe is eighty-five years old, and without the elevator he'd never be able to live in his apartment.

Pappa Joe is waiting by the open door.

He has blue eyes that twinkle, and he is so short that I can easily reach his face to kiss him.

Right away he brings out a plate of brownies, and we eat them, looking at the view from the living-room window.

My great-grandpa Joe is very independent. He shops in
the supermarket and cooks his own food. He reads, watches
television, and visits his friends and Grandma Sarah's sister
and brother, who live in the same building. He likes to take
long walks when the weather is good, and he is very good
at repairing things. He always teases us by saying, "I'll only
come to visit if there's something to fix or it's somebody's
birthday!"

"Pappa Joe," Daddy asks, "how has Grandma Sarah been feeling?"

Pappa Joe just smiles and says, "Okay."

Daddy tells me that every day Pappa Joe goes to the nursing home. He helps Grandma Sarah get dressed and then he helps her eat her meals. He loves Grandma Sarah very much, but she is too weak to be at home.

Mom stands up. "It's time for us to go," she says. She doesn't look too happy.

I remember Grandma Sarah a little before she got sick. She was very lively and she always made a lot of jokes in a loud voice. But that was a long time ago. Usually, only Mom and Daddy go to visit her. Now I feel a little scared.

Daddy says, "Pappa Joe, how about showing some photographs of Grandma Sarah to Kenny and Debbie before we leave?"

Pappa Joe goes to a closet and pulls out an album. It looks very old, and it's dusty.

"I don't feel like it now," I say.

Pappa Joe nods. "Later is fine."

We walk to the nursing home from Pappa Joe's.

It's a new-looking building with flowers all around. Some people are sitting in the sun in wheelchairs. Others are walking with canes. I try not to stare as we go inside and wait in a place called the visiting day room while Pappa Joe goes to get Grandma Sarah. Mom smiles at me, but I still feel scared.

Pappa Joe comes back, pushing an old lady in a wheelchair.

Is this my Grandma Sarah? She looks very tired and doesn't even say hello. I don't think she knows who we are. She just says "Joe, Joe" in that same loud voice I remember, and other things in a language I don't understand.

Mom and Daddy both speak softly to Grandma Sarah, but she doesn't answer. I look at Kenny, and he shrugs. We sit without speaking while Pappa Joe helps Grandma Sarah eat her lunch, and then, because she is sleepy, he takes her back to her room.

We walk slowly back to Pappa Joe's apartment building. Pappa Joe goes upstairs with Mom, and when they come down he has the album. I'm glad it's time to go home. I'm not afraid of seeing Grandma Sarah anymore, but it is sad that she doesn't remember who I am.

Mom says, "We'll all feel better when we've had something to eat."

We get home just in time. All my grandmas and grandpas arrive with my Uncle Steve. Daddy starts the barbecue. Kenny and I help set the table. Everyone has brought food. Mom and I bring out the salads and other dishes, and Kenny carries glasses of iced tea, soda, and juice. There is hardly room on the table for our plates.

Finally, we sit down. The food is so good! There's a lot of talking and laughing, and when all the food is eaten everyone helps clear the table.

While the others settle down to talk, Mom and I get the dessert ready. I've been thinking about Grandma Sarah all through lunch. "Why doesn't she know who we are?" I ask.

Mom answers very seriously. "Grandma Sarah's mind really isn't in this world anymore. She may be thinking and remembering many lovely things, but she can't tell us what they are."

"Is she close to heaven now?"

Mom smiles and gives me a hug. "I think she's very close to heaven, and we all have wonderful memories of her to share. Go get the album and see if Pappa Joe would like to look at it now."

I don't need to be told twice! I run to find the album and bring it to Pappa Joe. Even Kenny is interested in the old photographs. While we're looking at them, the whole family talks about my great-grandma Sarah.

Grandma Sarah is a special person. She was born in Russia and she came to America and married Pappa Joe when they were both very young. Grandma Sarah always worked hard, raising her children and sewing dresses in a factory. She was poor and she wanted the best for her family and for other poor people too. She joined unions, worked in politics, and marched in many parades. Today she would be called an activist.

Also, Grandma Sarah was a great cook. Everyone remembers her desserts. The whole family would pick blueberries in the country for Grandma Sarah's blueberry pies, and she loved to mix jello with nuts or applesauce or other surprising ingredients. All the big family dinners were held in her house—until she got too tired—and she always served three kinds of cake.

But best of all were the discussions, all the relatives yelling and arguing over what they believed was right. Now, my grandmas and grandpas say, the dinners are not the same: They are just too quiet!

As I put the album aside, I hope that Mom is right, and that in her mind Grandma Sarah is in a lovely place.

Pappa Joe is very quiet. Daddy asks him about his friend Harry, and Pappa Joe takes out a postcard that Harry sent after he moved to Florida. Many of Pappa Joe's friends have moved to a warm climate. Their children and grandchildren visit when they can. But Pappa Joe decided to stay here, in the city where he and Grandma Sarah lived most of their lives. Sometimes he goes to Florida for a short vacation, but mostly he stays at home.

There's a photograph in the album of Pappa Joe when he was a young man. Kenny asks what Pappa Joe did then. Pappa Joe's eyes twinkle as he tells us about the ironworks factory where he worked, making gates and furniture and decorations for buildings. "That's why I'm so strong today. During the Depression—"

"When was that, Pappa Joe?"

"About fifty years ago. I couldn't get factory work. So I delivered ice. Refrigerators weren't invented yet, and people kept food in something called an icebox. I delivered big blocks of ice in five-, ten-, and twenty-five-cent pieces. That was a lot of money then! After the Depression, I went back to the ironworks factory."

"But you never stopped wanting to learn new things," Daddy adds. "Remember, in your sixties, you took driving lessons for the first time."

"Yes," agrees Pappa Joe, "and I got my license, but I drove so fast that Grandma Sarah refused to get in the car with me!"

Everyone is laughing. Mom and Daddy bring out dessert and we pull our chairs into a circle on the patio.

Pappa Joe likes to relax now because he worked so hard when he was younger. But not all older people want to retire. One of my grandmas reminds us that Ronald Reagan was elected president when he was sixty-nine.

"And George Washington was fifty-seven when *he* was elected," Kenny adds.

Not everyone wants to be president, of course. A lot of older people are like our neighbors who garden and jog for health and for fun.

We're all trying to top each other with stories. One of my grandpas tells us that Colonel Sanders was over sixty when he started Kentucky Fried Chicken. Grandma Moses began painting when she was almost eighty. Not only that, Jack LaLanne proved he could pull a boat through the water with his teeth when he was seventy! It's true, what Pappa Joe always says: Older people can choose many ways to live, as long as they are healthy.

Lunch is over and it's time for the grandmas and grandpas to go home. We kiss them good-bye, saying, "See you very soon!"

Pappa Joe winks at me and heads straight for the basement. He knows I've been hoping he would help me fix my dollhouse. Upstairs, I can hear my mother and father talking in the kitchen, but downstairs Pappa Joe and I work quietly, hardly saying a word.

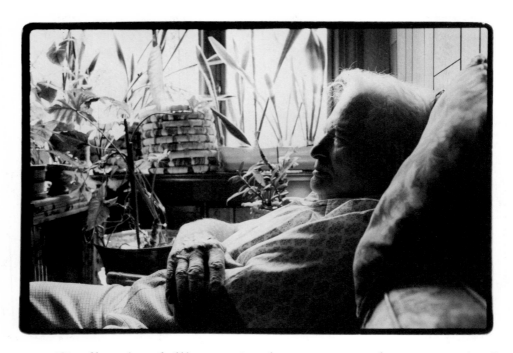

Finally, the dollhouse is almost as good as new. As I carry it to my room, Pappa Joe settles down in our big living-room chair. I know he's going to take a nap, and when he wakes up we'll go to visit Marco.

Marco is Pappa Joe's old friend. They used to live a few blocks apart. But when Marco's wife died, he decided he didn't want to live alone. So he moved to our neighborhood, to a building near the ocean where people his age live together. He has his own room, but he eats his meals in a large dining room with his friends and can join in many activities if he wants to. Marco is a good neighbor for us to have.

Pappa Joe and I walk together to Marco's home. Marco is waiting on the front porch, and he and Pappa Joe shake hands and hug each other.

I run down the boardwalk while he and Pappa Joe
stroll and talk. It's getting near suppertime and they say
good-night, a little sadly because they can't see each other
as often as they used to.

Soon it will be time for Pappa Joe to go home. Sometimes I wish he could live with us, but I know he'd rather live on his own. We have supper, and then Daddy gets out the car. Pappa Joe can't stay any longer, because he has to get up early tomorrow to be with Grandma Sarah. He kisses me and says, "Sweet dreams." I wave until the car is out of sight.

Later, I look through the album again. I think about how much I love Pappa Joe. I hope I see him again soon.